PEANUTS®

Here Comes the EASTER BEAGLE!

By Charles M. Schulz

Adapted by Jason Cooper

Illustrated by Robert Pope

SIMON SPOTLIGHT
An imprint of Simon & Schuster Children's Publishing Division
New York London Toronto Sydney New Delhi
1230 Avenue of the Americas, New York, New York 10020
This Simon Spotlight paperback edition January 2018
© 2018 Peanuts Worldwide LLC
SIMON SPOTLIGHT and colophon are registered trademarks of Simon & Schuster, Inc.
For information about special discounts for bulk purchases, please contact Simon & Schuster Special Sales at
1-866-506-1949 or business@simonandschuster.com.
Manufactured in the United States of America 1018 LAK
4 6 8 10 9 7 5 3
ISBN 978-1-5344-1016-9 (pbk)
ISBN 978-1-5344-1017-6 (eBook)

Linus and his brother Rerun are at home, staring anxiously out the window. "The Easter Beagle will be here any moment," Linus tells his little brother. "He will bring Easter cheer and beautifully colored eggs to all the boys and girls . . . even if he is a little late."

"A little late?" Lucy says to her little brothers. "You've been waiting hours for that lousy beagle. He's probably too busy imagining he's a famous pilot or a race car driver to deliver eggs. You're wasting a perfectly good Easter staring out the window."

"You're right," Linus says. "Let's wait outside, Rerun."

Outside, Linus and Rerun see their friend Pigpen. "Pigpen, are you waiting for the Easter Beagle, too?" Rerun asks.

"Yes! I can't wait to see him," Pigpen says, pulling an old rotten egg out of his pocket. "And once he gives me a new egg, I can eat the one he gave me last year!"

Soon more friends arrive. "I hope he gets here soon," says Franklin.
"So do I," Marcie says. "I still haven't learned how to make Easter eggs!"
Rerun sighs. "He sure seems to be taking a long time to get here."
"Don't worry, Rerun," Linus tells him. "The Easter Beagle won't let us down.
In fact, I'll make sure of it!"

Linus leaves and finds Snoopy asleep on the roof of his doghouse. Charlie Brown is picking up Snoopy's breakfast dish.

"Why isn't your dog out delivering eggs?" Linus asks.

"Who cares? He never gives me any," Charlie Brown says.

"Snoopy! Wake up!" Linus shouts. "We're all waiting for the Easter Beagle!" Snoopy wakes with a start.

"Let's go, Snoopy!" Linus hollers. "You have to start delivering eggs!"

Snoopy doesn't look very good.

"Oh no," Linus says. "What's wrong?"

"I think he might be sick," Charlie Brown says.

I can't be the Easter Beagle today, Snoopy thinks.

"But we're counting on you, Snoopy!" Linus says. "What if I color the eggs, and you deliver them?"

Snoopy shrugs his shoulders. Linus rushes off to find some eggs to color.

Snoopy's friend Woodstock flutters down and lands beside him.

Snoopy holds his upset tummy. *Who knew that too much root beer could be a bad thing?* he thinks.

Before long, Linus returns with a basket full of colored eggs.

"Here you go, Snoopy!" Linus calls. "I've colored the eggs for you! All you have to do is hand them out."

Snoopy takes the basket of eggs and looks them over.

I don't know, Snoopy thinks. *I still don't feel well.*

"Here come Sally and Eudora, Easter Beagle. Try delivering an egg, and I bet you'll feel better!" Linus says.

Snoopy lazily tosses an egg over his shoulder.

The egg lands right on Eudora's head. "Hey!" she yells. "What an Easter Scrooge!"

Sally angrily walks over to Snoopy. "Listen here, Easter Beagle!" she says. "If Eudora gets some eggs, then so do I! Cough 'em up!"

Snoopy dumps the whole basket of eggs over Sally's head.

Happy Easter, he thinks. Then he trudges home to go back to bed.

"Good grief," says Sally, "I hope he's not the Birthday Beagle too!"

Linus sighs sadly. "This isn't right," he says. "The Easter Beagle is supposed to bring joy to all children. He is supposed to spread the spirit of spring, not make everyone feel crummy. Maybe it's better if the Easter Beagle doesn't come this year."

Woodstock flies over to the empty Easter egg basket and chirps at Linus.

"Really, Woodstock?" Linus asks Woodstock. "You'll deliver the eggs?"
Woodstock chirps loudly.

"I don't know," Linus says. "Are you sure you're up to the task? Can you spread the joy of spring the way a beagle can?"

Woodstock pops a pair of bunny ears on his head in response.

"Wonderful!" Linus says. "I'll go color more eggs!"

Rerun, still waiting for the Easter Beagle, is starting to worry. "Maybe Lucy was right," he tells Pigpen. "Maybe the Easter Beagle isn't going to come this year."

"It looks that way," Pigpen says. He looks at the old stinky egg in his hand and places it carefully back into his pocket. "Oh well," he says, "I suppose I can wait until next year to eat this. . . ."

Lucy joins the others outside. "Stop waiting for that silly beagle, everyone," she says. "Go home and eat the ears off a chocolate bunny!"

Rerun looks at Lucy sadly and says, "Linus promised I'd get an egg from the Easter Beagle. . . ."

"Hey, what's that?" Franklin asks, pointing down the road.

"It's the Easter Beagle . . . I mean, the Easter Beagle's assistant!" Linus says.

The kids cheer. Woodstock delivers eggs to everyone, even Lucy, who smiles shyly.

And Charlie Brown, who never got an egg from the Easter Beagle, gets one from the Easter Beagle's assistant.

Woodstock even places a pair of fuzzy bunny ears on Linus. "Where does he keep getting these ears?" Linus wonders.

Woodstock has one last delivery to make. Even the Easter Beagle enjoys receiving an Easter egg.
Snoopy hugs Woodstock tightly and thinks, *Happy Easter, little friend.*

HAPPY EASTER

©2018 PNTS

Happy Easter

©2018 PNTS

EASTER BEAGLE

HIP HOP HOORAY!

HIP HOP HOORAY!

EGG-CELLENT

HAPPY EASTER